THE THREE BEARS

PAUL GALDONE

CLARION BOOKS / NEW YORK

Clarion Books
a Houghton Mifflin Company imprint
215 Park Avenue South, New York, NY 10003
Copyright © 1972 by Paul Galdone

PA ISBN 0-89919-401-X   ISBN: 0-395-28811-8.
Library of Congress Catalog Card Number: 78-158833.
Book designed by Paul Galdone. Printed in the U.S.A. All rights reserved.

BBN   23

Once upon a time there were Three Bears who lived together in a house of their own in the woods.

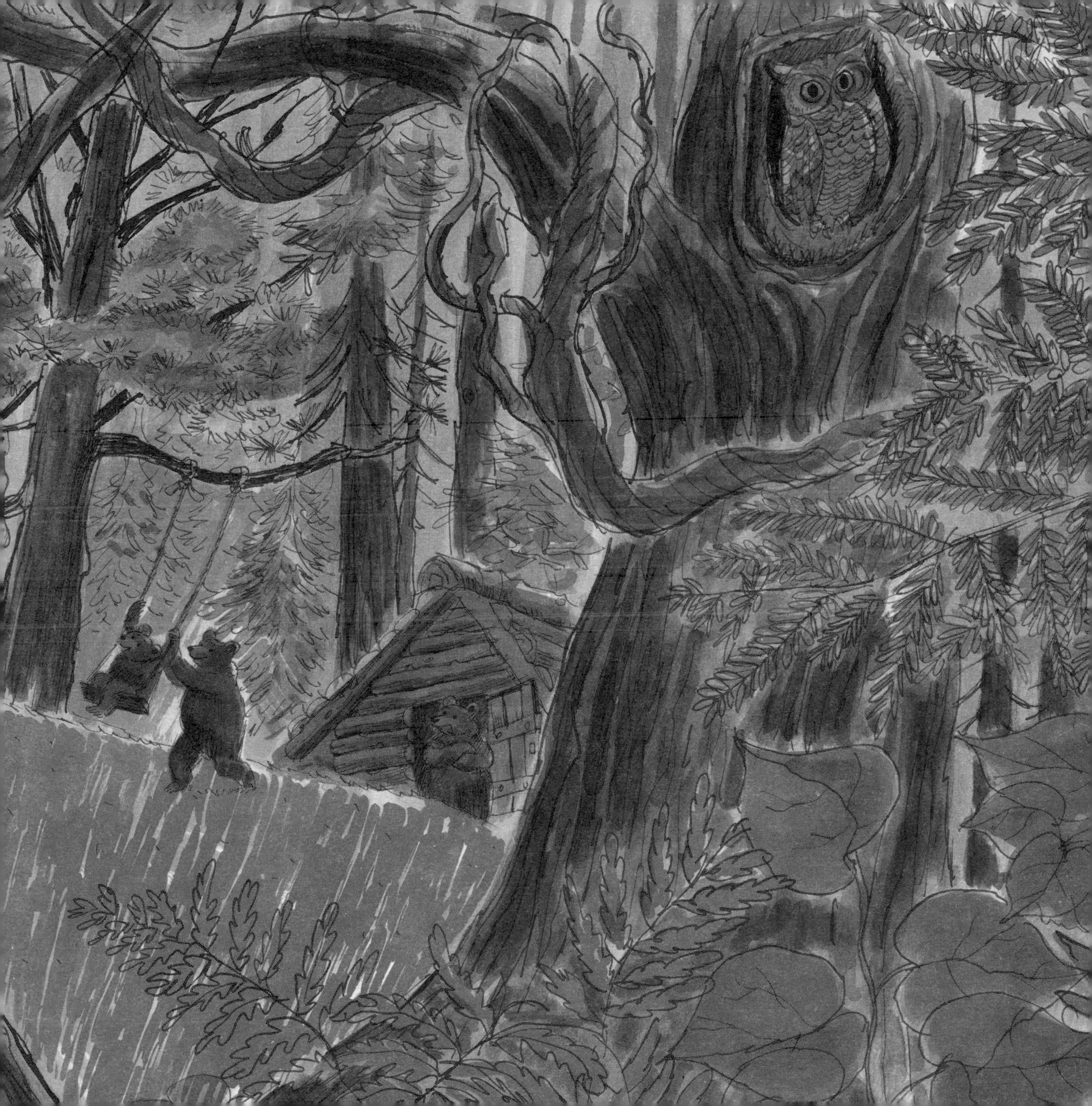

one was
a Middle-Sized Bear,

One of them was
a Little Wee Bear,

and the other was
a Great Big Bear.

They each had a bowl for their porridge.

The Little Wee Bear
had a little wee bowl,

the Middle-Sized Bear
had a middle-sized bowl,

and the Great Big Bear
had a great big bowl.

They each had a chair to sit in.

The Little Wee Bear
had a little wee chair,

the Middle-Sized Bear
had a middle-sized chair,

and the Great Big Bear
had a great big chair.

And they each had a bed to sleep in.

The Little Wee Bear
had a little wee bed,

the Middle-Sized Bear
had a middle-sized bed,

and the Great Big Bear
had a great big bed.

One morning, the Three Bears
made porridge for breakfast
and poured it into their bowls.
But it was too hot to eat.
So they decided to go
for a walk in the woods
until it cooled.

While the Three Bears were walking,

a little girl named Goldilocks
came to their house.

10

First she looked in at the window,

and then she peeked through the keyhole.

Of course there was nobody inside.
Goldilocks turned the handle of the door.

The door was not locked, because
the Three Bears were trusting bears.
They did no one any harm, and never
thought anyone would harm them.

So Goldilocks opened the door and went right in.

There was the porridge
on the table.
It smelled very, very good!

Goldilocks didn't stop to think whose porridge it was.
She went straight to it.

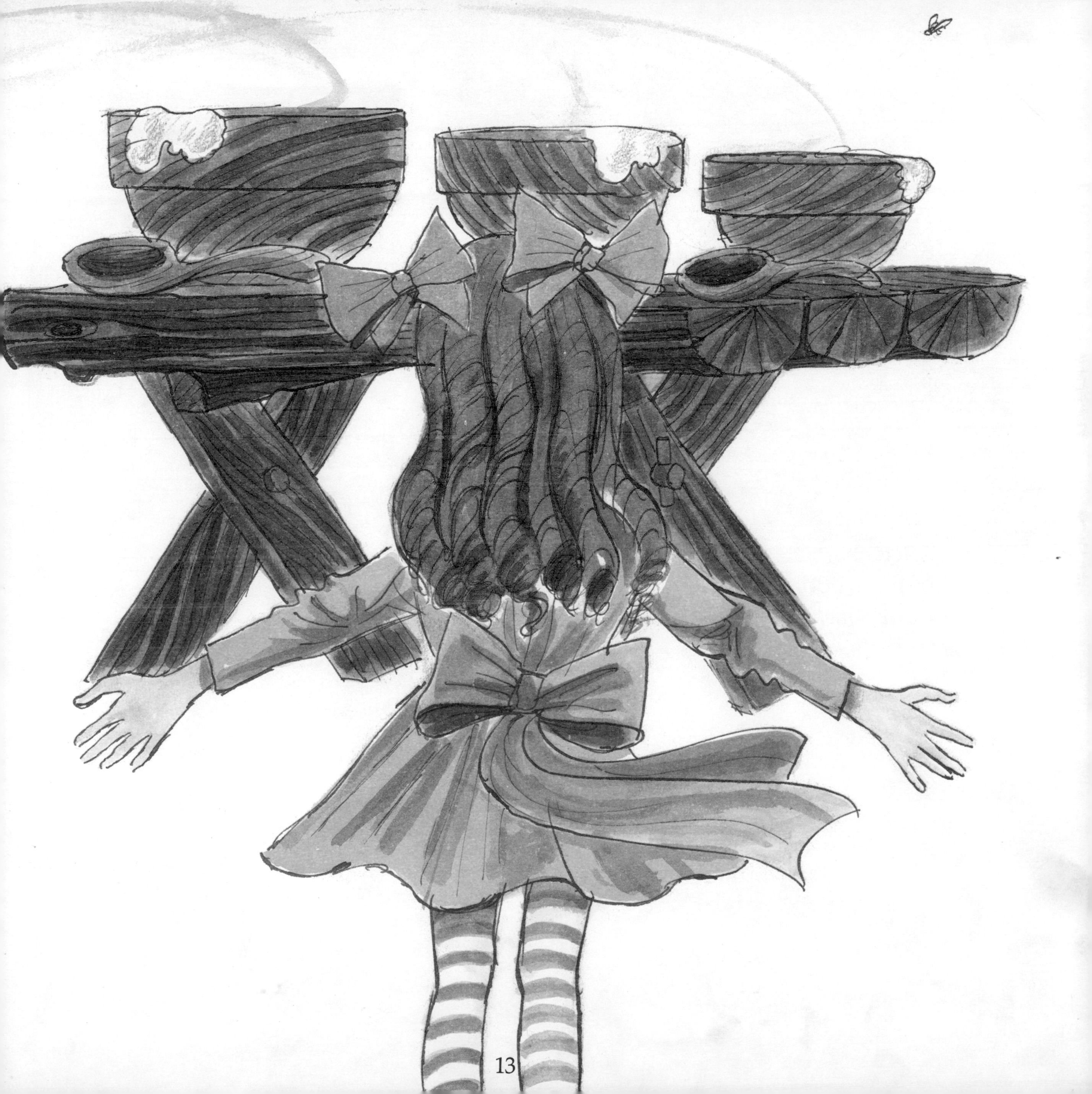

First she tasted the porridge
of the Great Big Bear.
But it was too hot.

Then she tasted the porridge
of the Middle-Sized Bear.
But it was too cold.

Then she tasted the porridge
of the Little Wee Bear.

14

It was neither too hot nor too cold, but just right. Goldilocks liked it so much that she ate it all up.

Then Goldilocks went into the parlor to see what else she could find.

There were the three chairs.

First she sat down in the chair
of the Great Big Bear.
But it was too hard.

Then she sat down in the chair
of the Middle-Sized Bear.
But it was too soft.

Then she sat down in the chair
of the Little Wee Bear.
It was neither too hard
nor too soft, but just right.
Goldilocks liked it so much
that she rocked and rocked,

until ...

the bottom of the chair fell out!
Down she went—plump!—onto the floor.

Goldilocks went into the bedroom
where the Three Bears slept.

17

First she lay down upon the bed
of the Great Big Bear.
But it was too high at the head for her.

Then she lay down upon the bed
of the Middle-Sized Bear.
But it was too high at the foot for her.

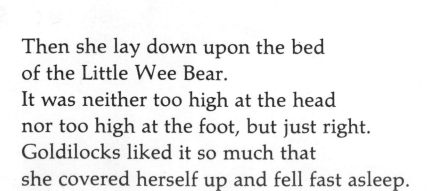

Then she lay down upon the bed
of the Little Wee Bear.
It was neither too high at the head
nor too high at the foot, but just right.
Goldilocks liked it so much that
she covered herself up and fell fast asleep.

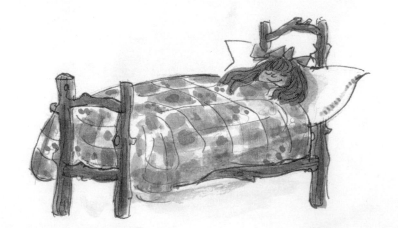

By this time,
the Three Bears thought
their porridge
would be cool enough.

So they came home
for breakfast.

Goldilocks had left
the spoon of the Great Big Bear
in his porridge bowl.
He noticed it, first thing.

"SOMEBODY HAS BEEN
TASTING MY PORRIDGE!"
said the Great Big Bear
in his great big voice.

Goldilocks had left
the spoon of the Middle-Sized Bear
in her porridge bowl, too.

"SOMEBODY HAS BEEN TASTING MY PORRIDGE!"
said the Middle-Sized Bear
in her middle-sized voice.

21

Then the Little Wee Bear looked at his bowl.

"SOMEBODY HAS BEEN TASTING MY PORRIDGE
AND HAS EATEN IT ALL UP!"
cried the Little Wee Bear
in his little wee voice.

The Three Bears went
into the parlor.

22

Goldilocks had left
the cushion crooked
in the chair
of the Great Big Bear.
He noticed it, first thing.

"SOMEBODY HAS BEEN
SITTING IN MY CHAIR!"
said the Great Big Bear
in his great big voice.

23

Goldilocks had squashed down the cushion
in the chair of the Middle-Sized Bear.

"SOMEBODY HAS BEEN SITTING IN MY CHAIR!"
said the Middle-Sized Bear
in her middle-sized voice.

Then the Little Wee Bear looked at his chair.

"SOMEBODY HAS BEEN SITTING IN MY CHAIR
AND HAS SAT RIGHT THROUGH IT!"
cried the Little Wee Bear
in his little wee voice.

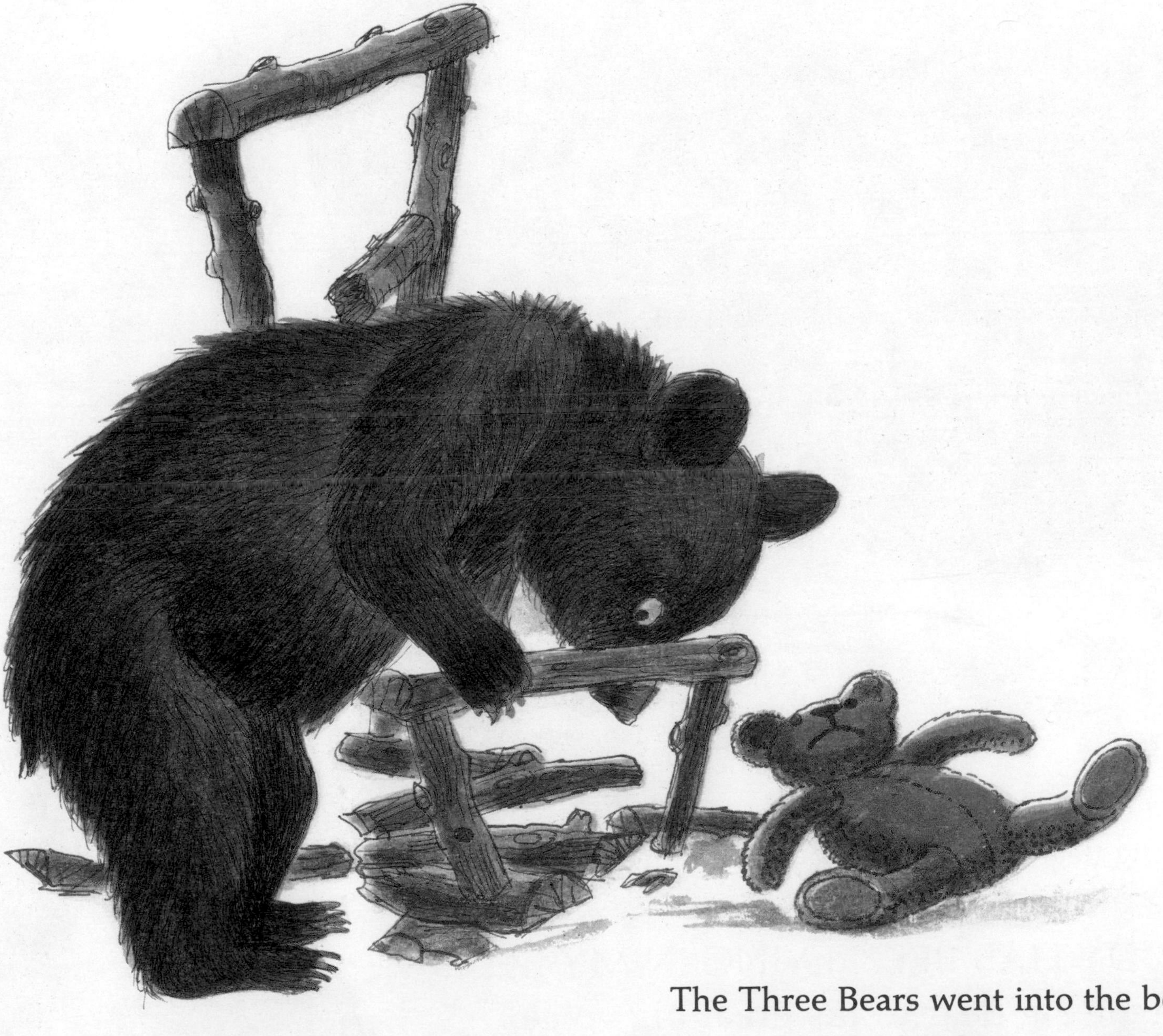

The Three Bears went into the bedroom.

Goldilocks had pulled the pillow
of the Great Big Bear out of place.
He noticed it, first thing.

"SOMEBODY HAS BEEN LYING IN MY BED!"
said the Great Big Bear in his great big voice.

26

Goldilocks had pulled the blanket
of the Middle-Sized Bear out of place.

"SOMEBODY HAS BEEN LYING IN MY BED!"
said the Middle-Sized Bear
in her middle-sized voice.

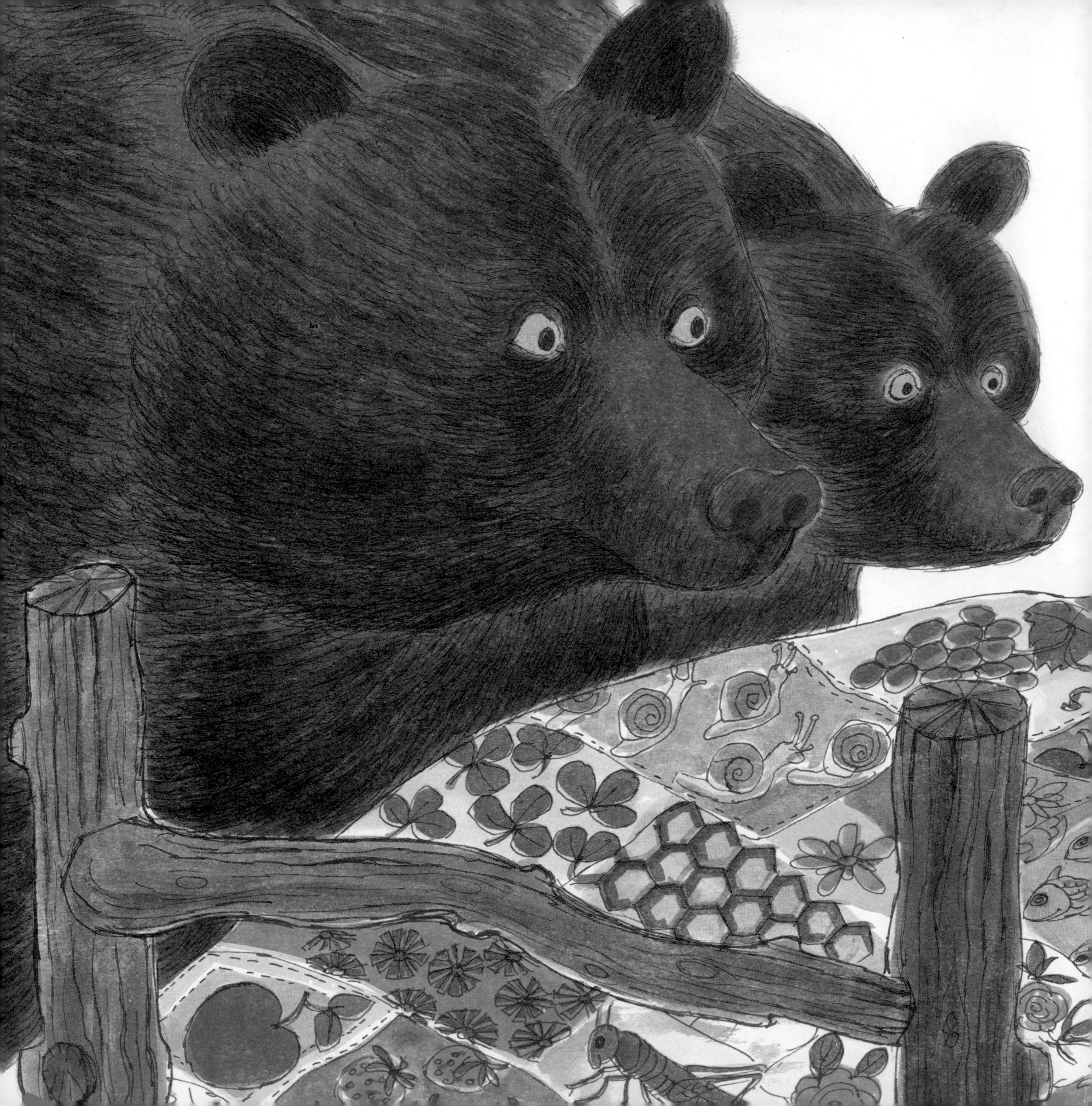

Then the Little Wee Bear looked at his bed.

"SOMEBODY HAS BEEN LYING IN MY BED—AND HERE SHE IS!"
cried the Little Wee Bear in his little wee voice.

This woke Goldilocks up at once. There were the Three Bears all staring at her.

Goldilocks was so frightened that
she tumbled out of bed and ran to the open window.

Out she jumped!

And she ran away as fast
as she could, never looking behind her.

No one knows what happened to Goldilocks after that.

As for the Three Bears, they never saw her again.